Tales from Mossy Bottom Farm

ON THE BALL

First U.S. edition 2015

Library of Congress Catalog Card Number 2015936914
ISBN 978-0-7636-8059-6

15 16 17 18 19 20 BVG 10 9 8 7 6 5 4 3 2 1

Printed in Berryville, VA, U.S.A.

This book was typeset in Manticore.
The illustrations were created digitally.

Candlewick Entertainment
An imprint of Candlewick Press
99 Dover Street
Somerville, Massachusetts 02144

visit us at www.candlewick.com

Tales from Mossy Bottom Farm

ON THE BALL

Martin Howard

illustrated by Andy Janes

CANDLEWICK
ENTERTAINMENT

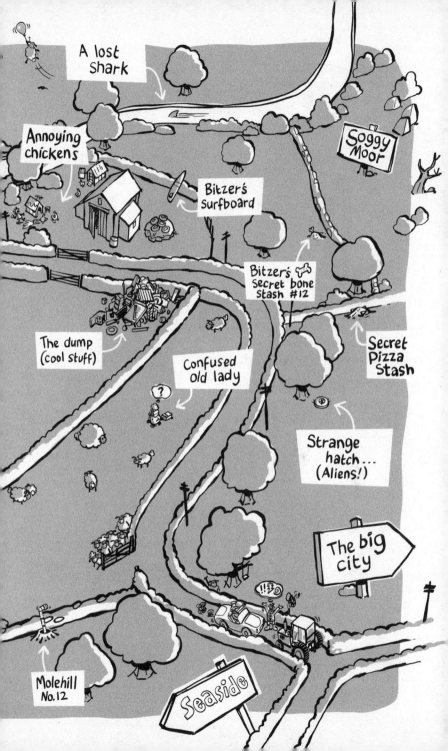

SHAUN is the leader of the Flock. He's clever, cool, and always keeps his head when the other sheep are losing theirs.

BITZER

The Farmer's faithful dog and a good friend to Shaun, Bitzer is an ever-suffering sheepdog, doing his best to keep Shaun's pals out of trouble.

THE FARMER

Running the farm with Bitzer at his side, the Farmer is completely oblivious to the human-like intelligence—or stupidity—of his flock.

THE FLOCK

One big happy (if slightly dopey) family, the sheep like to play and create mischief together, though it's usually Shaun and Bitzer who sort out the resulting messes.

THE PIGS

Mocking, lazy, and greedy, the pigs are always ruining Shaun's schemes and disrupting life on the farm.

DEREK THE FROG

He's famous in Florida and Sweden but doesn't like to croak about it. Enjoys bananas and smooth jazz.

CONTENTS

CHAPTER ONE

A GOOD SPORT

On Mossy Bottom Farm, the animals sweltered in the heat. The pigs rolled in mud to cool down, spouting muck like pink whales. Beneath the shade of the tree, the bull flicked at flies with his tail, snorting and glaring around as if to say, "It is never too hot for a pair of horns up the seat of the pants."

Only the ducks looked cool. They were doing lazy backstrokes around the pond.

In the meadow, one or two of the sheep slowly munched grass. The rest of the Flock lay in the shade with their feet in the air, too hot and bored to even stand up.

The Farmer dozed in a deck chair by the farmhouse with a knotted handkerchief on his head. A newspaper fluttered gently on his face with every snore. The headline read, **MOSSY BOTTOM IS HOT, HOT, HOT: LADY TOFFINGTON-SNIVELY STEPS OUT IN HER BATHING SUIT AT THE SWIMMING POOL.** He'd fallen asleep with a glass of fizzy lemonade in his hand. A frog named Derek had hopped inside the glass and was leaning against the rim, enjoying the bubbly drink as if it were a cool Jacuzzi.

Shaun rested against the stone wall by the meadow, tossing an old tennis ball up and down with one hoof. He yawned as he looked around for something to do.

Bitzer was outside his doghouse, examining a bone. It was a *good* bone—far too good to chew. It was the type of bone that should be in a display case or mounted over the fireplace. A bone to be passed down through the family—

The tennis ball *boinked* off his hat.

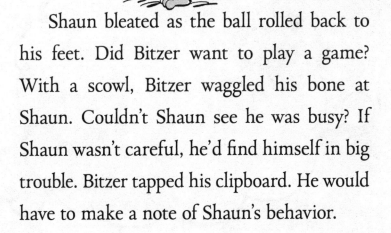

Shaun bleated as the ball rolled back to his feet. Did Bitzer want to play a game? With a scowl, Bitzer waggled his bone at Shaun. Couldn't Shaun see he was busy? If Shaun wasn't careful, he'd find himself in big trouble. Bitzer tapped his clipboard. He would have to make a note of Shaun's behavior.

Shaun grinned. Being in trouble sounded like fun. He picked up the ball and tossed it to Bitzer again.

Annoyed, Bitzer swung his bone. It hit the tennis ball with a plonk, sending it sailing across the meadow, where it dropped into Shirley's fleece. She blinked, reached in for the ball, nibbled it, then bleated at the sky. If it was going to rain strange objects, she would prefer a rain of ice cream, with sprinkles.

Bitzer's frown turned into a snicker. Hitting the ball had felt good. He crouched, panting as he swung the bone. Again! Again!

Shaun shook his head. Shirley had caught the ball, and that meant Bitzer was *out*. It was Shaun's turn with the bone.

Bitzer clutched the bone tightly and woofed. It wasn't fair. There weren't any rules, and it had just been a practice hit.

Shaun rolled his eyes and waved at Shirley. After giving the tennis ball one last nibble, just to make sure it wasn't ice cream, Shirley nudged it back. Shaun stopped it with a hoof and turned to Bitzer. OK, now they were playing properly. Was he ready?

Bitzer nodded: *Ready.*

Shaun windmilled his arm and let fly. The ball swished through the air . . .

THWACK!

As Bitzer watched the ball whizz across the blue sky, his inner dog took over: Fetch! He tossed the bone aside and, with his tongue lolling out, chased after the ball. Just before the ball hit the ground, he dived to catch it between his teeth.

Bursting with pride, Bitzer turned back, bowed, and woofed through a mouthful of tennis ball. How was *that*?

Shaun clapped, then picked up the bone. It was an excellent catch, and Bitzer was *out*!

The ball dropped from Bitzer's mouth. *Out*? He couldn't be out.

Shaun crossed his arms and tutted. If the ball was caught, the player who had hit it with the bone was out. Now it was *definitely* Shaun's turn.

By now, the Twins had wandered over. They both bleated and pointed toward the meadow. Perhaps the person with the bone should run around some bases while someone else fetched the ball.

Bitzer nodded enthusiastically and scribbled the new rule on his clipboard.

The day wasn't looking quite so boring anymore, Shaun thought a few minutes later, standing by a flowerpot and swinging Bitzer's bone.

The Twins had arranged four more flowerpots around the meadow in a diamond, with a fifth in the middle marking the place for the player throwing the ball. The rules were simple: Shaun had to hit the ball and try to run around all the flowerpots. The other team could get him out by dropping the ball into a flowerpot before he touched it.

Bitzer took his place as pitcher and glanced back at the Twins. Were they ready? He wound up to throw Shaun a zinger. As the Twins bleated, Bitzer let fly.

The ball zoomed across the meadow, making a zoommm noise.

By his flowerpot, Shaun squeezed his eyes closed and swung the bone. Thwack! The ball rose into the air and soared across the meadow with the Twins close behind.

With one eye on the Twins, Shaun sprinted past the first flowerpot, then the second. The Twins had caught up with the ball and were tossing it back. Could Shaun get to the third flowerpot? He'd give it his best shot.

His hoof touched the pot a second before Bitzer tossed the old tennis ball into it. Shaun was safe! He blew a raspberry at Bitzer.

Shaun wiped sweat out of his eyes and

looked around. What could he do now? He was stuck at the third flowerpot, and there was no one else on his team.

Hazel bleated to get his attention. Could she join his team?

She'd also had a really good idea for a water obstacle: Shaun bleated in delight as she turned on the tap at the corner of the meadow. A sprinkler whirled into action between the third and fourth flowerpots.

When Hazel swung the bone, she whacked the ball far out into the meadow, past the fielding Twins.

With a bleat of triumph, Shaun ran, grinning as he trotted through the sprinkler. He touched the last flowerpot. He was home, so his team had scored one run!

Curious, more sheep had turned up to see what was going on. Nuts raised a hoof while hopping up and down as if he needed to go to the bathroom. Could he be on a team too?

Bitzer nodded. Nuts could be on his team. And the hopping was a good idea; everyone should hop between the flowerpots. Hurriedly, Bitzer scribbled the new rule down on his clipboard.

Shaun frowned. Bitzer, the Twins, and Nuts made four. He and Hazel made two. His team needed more players.

The rest of the Flock bleated. They all wanted to play. Timmy's Mum was already knitting Timmy a special hat for . . . for . . . She looked up, bleating. What was the game called?

Bitzer scribbled on his clipboard, then showed it to the Flock. It read, **BITZER'S BONE, BALL, AND FLOWERPOT GAME WITH ADDED WATER SPRINKLERS.** Shaun shook his head. The name

wasn't quite right. Perhaps it should be called the **FARMYARD SUMMER HOP**.... No, that sounded like a dance. Shirley bleated. **SHIRLEYBALL** was nice. Shaun stuck his tongue out at her. If they were going to name it after someone, it should be after the sheep who invented it, so it would be **SHAUNBALL**.

Hazel interrupted with an impatient bleat. Since they were hopping around and around the field, they could call it **ROUNDERS**....

13

"Heh, heh, heh," Bitzer snickered. He held up the clipboard, showing a fresh page. At the top was written, **THE RULES OF BITZERBALL.** Underneath, in Bitzer's large handwriting, it read, **RULE 1: THE RULES CAN CHANGE AT ANY TIME.**

Shaun sighed. The name didn't really matter. They could spend all day arguing about it, or just play.

CHAPTER TWO
THE TRIPLE BOINGER

Shaun gritted his teeth and took a practice swing with the bone. With the teams chosen, they had decided to start a new game. A turnip had been flipped to see which side batted first, and Shaun's team had won.

Bitzer's players were in their fielding positions, which Nuts had marked out on the clipboard. They were named **SILLY, SLIGHTLY SILLY,** and **DEEPLY SILLY.** Nuts had chosen to play in the **COMPLETELY BONKERS** position, so he was wearing a pair of the Farmer's underpants on his head, as required in the official rules — which by now were twelve pages long.

Hoping he could remember all the rules, especially since they kept changing, Shaun turned and waggled his bottom at Bitzer. (RULE 42: THE PLAYER HOLDING THE BONE SIGNALS THAT HE OR SHE IS READY BY WAVING HIS OR HER BACKSIDE AT THE PITCHER.)

At the pitcher's flowerpot, Bitzer blew his whistle. Then he blew on the ball and polished it on his chest. His eyes met Shaun's. Bitzer pulled back his arm and hurled the ball.

It cannoned out of his paw, bounced off a molehill, and shot off again, straight toward Shaun.

TWAPPP! Bone met ball.

Shaun saw one of the Twins weaving across the meadow, pushing an old doll's stroller he had found on the dump. (**RULE 38: IF A FIELDER CATCHES A BALL IN THE STROLLER OF WHOOPS, THE WHOLE TEAM IS OUT.**) Shaun grinned as the Twin crashed into Nuts, who fell onto the stroller, crushing it flat. Wheels spun off in all directions.

Plop! The tennis ball bounced in front of Nuts's nose and rolled away under a bush. Nuts blinked at it, dazed.

With a grin, Shaun hopped as fast as he could, quickly passing the first, second, and third flowerpots.

Behind him, his teammates bleated. Keep going!

Nuts dived into the bush. Shaun could see his back legs wiggling in the air as he searched for the ball. Ahead was the lawn sprinkler. Shaun hopped through the spray, giggling as cool water soaked him. He was almost home. Was he going to make it? He glanced over his shoulder to see if Nuts had retrieved the ball, and—

Timmy spat out his pacifier and gave Shaun a reproachful bleat.

Shaun bleated a sheepish apology as he scrambled to his hooves.

Nuts had thrown the ball straight toward Bitzer, who was waiting by the final flowerpot.

Heart in his mouth, Shaun hopped for his life, then threw himself at the flowerpot. He skidded along the grass on his stomach, touching the pot with the tip of his hoof.

His team went wild, making up another rule on the spot. Any player who, like Shaun, made it past every flowerpot all at once earned a **BITZERBALL CHEER**.

As the bleats faded away, Timmy's Mum kept on cheering. She kicked her legs in the air while waving her hooves. She was having so much fun that she made up a little song, which went something like, "Two, four, six, eight, Shaun's team will DOMINATE! Bitzerball, Bitzerball, BITZERBALL!" She wanted something to wave. Something fluffy would be best. . . .

Hearing excited bleating, Shaun looked over his shoulder.

A rabbit in each front hoof, Timmy's Mum danced her way across the meadow.

By the gate, Mower Mouth the goat bleated through a mouthful of knotted handkerchief that he had nibbled off the snoozing Farmer's head. The ducks had wandered over, and one quacked—a sure sign of high excitement. Even the pigs were leaning on the wall, pointing and squealing to one another.

Chuckling to himself, Shaun took a bow. Bitzerball was *fantastic!*

Meanwhile, Bitzer scribbled yet another new rule on his clipboard: the **TIMMY OBSTACLE.** The fielding team could ask Timmy to sit wherever they pleased in an attempt to trip players on the batting team.

Next up to bat was Shirley. After taking the bone, she shook her bottom at Bitzer. The ball flew from Bitzer's hand, and Shirley smacked it with a loud grunt. . . .

23

With a loud "Whh-wha-wha?" the Farmer jumped to his feet. He glared around to see who was throwing things at snoozing farmers.

In the meadow, sheep munched grass. In the yard, chickens pecked dirt. Bitzer leaned against the gate, studying his clipboard. Mower Mouth the goat swallowed the shredded remains of the Farmer's handkerchief.

"Huurrrumph," harrumphed the Farmer. Then he said, "Bah," and tossed the tennis ball over his shoulder into the pigsty before heading into the farmhouse for a fresh glass of lemonade.

Shaun breathed a sigh of relief and patted Shirley. The water sprinkler fell out of her fleece.

All around the field, sheep stepped
away from the flowerpots they had been
hiding. With the Farmer gone, the pigs were
squealing again. Shaun glanced over and
saw them swinging a branch at the tennis

ball. Shaun beamed. A sheep-versus-pigs **BITZERBALL** match would be even *more* fun.

The pigs always cheat, but this time they wouldn't understand the rules. Shaun's smile turned into a chuckle as he imagined the penalties the Flock could make up.

Hooves clasped behind his back, he strolled over to the pigsty and nodded toward the meadow. Would the pigs like to play a match against the Flock?

The pigs oinked and grunted in reply. The sheep wouldn't stand a chance. Challenge accepted!

Shaun nodded. The sheep would find a way to keep the Farmer busy. Tomorrow, they would play.

Squeeee! One pig held up a hoof. Just one thing. Since the sheep had made up so many rules, it was only fair that the pigs add a few of their own.

CHAPTER THREE
PIGS, PIGS, PIGS

An owl hooted. In the moonlight, Shaun stood on Hazel's shoulders. She was standing on Nuts's shoulders, who was standing on the Twins' shoulders, who were standing on Shirley.

Bitzer woofed nervously, twisting his hat in his paws. Like most of Shaun's plans, this one could easily go horribly wrong. Bitzer didn't like playing tricks on the Farmer, but the **BITZERBALL** game was just too exciting. Besides, the Farmer had been looking a little tired recently. Some extra sleep would be good for him.

It was a warm night, so the bedroom window was open. Shaun carefully parted the curtains and peered in. The Farmer was in the middle of a dream. His glasses glinted on the bedside table, next to the alarm clock.

Shaun bleated quietly. Hoof by hoof, the Flock passed a long stick up to him. Frowning with concentration, Shaun carefully poked it through the window toward the bedside table, trying to hold it steady as the sheep underneath him swayed . . .

Tinkle. The Farmer's glasses fell to the floor.

"Gurraaupppafaarrr," the Farmer mumbled in his sleep.

Shaun ducked under the windowsill. When everything was quiet again, Shaun peeked into the room again.

"Hummanaaahhum-an-ahh," muttered the Farmer. Then he sat bolt upright in bed and punched the air with his fist. He shouted thanks to an audience that existed only in his dream before dropping back to the pillow with a loud snore.

Sighing with relief, Shaun grinned. The Farmer was obviously dreaming that he was a rock star.

Tongue sticking out of the corner of his mouth, Shaun poked the branch in through the window again. Then he used it to turn the hands of the clock backward: one hour, two hours, three hours, four hours, five hours, six hours. . . . Then Shaun set the clock back another six hours. It was best to be on the safe side.

The Farmer was dealt with. Now to beat the pigs!

* * *

Shading his eyes from the sun, Shaun gazed around the field in horror. The flowerpots were still in place, but everything else looked very different. The pigs were gathered around the first flowerpot. The lawn sprinkler was gone from the second one, but its hose had turned the grass into an oozing swamp. A heap of straw had been piled up at the third.

With a smug oink, the pig captain handed Bitzer a hoof full of mud-stained pages covered in wobbly writing. The pigs' new rules. The first one was that **BITZERBALL** would now be called **PIGGY STOMP.**

Shaun bleated in protest. The pigs couldn't do that. The captain jabbed a hoof at the Flock's original rules. **RULE 1: THE RULES CAN CHANGE AT ANY TIME.** Underneath, a new rule had been written in tiny letters. It stated that when the Flock lost, they would have to bleat the **"PIGS, PIGS, PIGS"** song every time they saw a pig for the next month.

The song lyrics had been helpfully attached, on a separate wad of paper. Feeling faint, Shaun clutched his forehead and peered at the mud-spattered first verse:

Oh, pigs, pigs, pigs, so awesome and groovy,
As handsome and cool as stars in a movie!
At sports and games they never fail;
Sheep can kiss their curly tails.

There were another sixty-eight verses.

Pages flew.

Shaun's eyes darted this way and that as he scanned more new rules. The pigs had added obstacles for the players to complete at

the four flowerpots. And there was no longer any batting. Instead, players had to carry the ball around the course and then drop it into the flowerpot at the end. And the pigs had made sure that the obstacles were much easier for pigs than sheep.

Shaun bleated in frustration. The game had completely changed. . . .

Bitzer shrugged. **RULE 1** was clear. The pigs hadn't done anything wrong.

The pig captain snickered as he pointed out another new rule. **RULE 86: IF THE FLOCK DIDN'T WANT TO PLAY, THEY COULD PLAY THE SQUEALING PIGGY CARD AND FORFEIT THE GAME.** He began squealing. *Oh, pigs, pigs, pigs . . .*

Bitzer interrupted with a loud peep on his whistle. He looked at Shaun. Were they ready, or did he wish to play the **SQUEALING PIGGY** card?

Shaun shook his head. No way. The pig captain oinked. Good. Now the Flock would need to choose their captain.

Shaun turned to see a forest of hooves in the air. Everyone wanted to lead the Flock to victory over the pigs. He bleated. Whom to choose?

Timmy was too small; his mom was needed to be in charge of the cheerleading; Shirley was . . . well . . . Shirley; the Twins would just argue if the Flock chose one of them and not the other; Nuts would almost certainly do something wrong and get every penalty in the rules. Hazel would be a sensible choice, though she had stubbed her hoof playing the day before and it might slow her down, which just left . . .

The Flock looked at one another, then cheered Shaun—their new captain.

Shaun blinked nervously at the obstacle course. Having read the pigs' new rules, he could now identify the obstacles he'd seen earlier. He would have to run through a maze at the first flowerpot, cross the **PIG-SWILL SWAMP** at the second, build a **HOUSE OF STRAW** at the third, and then sprint to the flowerpot at the end of the course. And the pigs had written more penalties into the rules than Shaun could count. The Flock couldn't forfeit the game, though, or they would have to sing the horrible **"PIGS, PIGS, PIGS"** song for a whole *month*. They had to win. But how?

Gulping, Shaun took the clipboard from Bitzer and flicked through the rules again. His eyes narrowed, and he nodded to himself as he found what he was looking for.

The old rules of **BITZERBALL** were almost buried beneath the pigs' new rules, but they were still there.

Shaun's frown turned into a smile. The game wasn't lost yet.

The pig captain snorted impatiently. Could they just get on with it and play?

Shaun nodded. He was ready.

According to the new rules, the captains would take turns to complete the **PIGGY STOMP** obstacles. The player to go first would be decided by the winner of a quick round of **HOOF, HOOF, SQUEAL, BLEAT.**

Bitzer counted for Shaun and the pig captain. Woof, woof, woof . . .

Shaun and the pig each held out a hoof. Bitzer checked the page. Pig hoof crushed sheep hoof. The pigs won.

The captain poked Shaun in the chest. *He* could go first. With a smug oink, the pig led his team out onto the field. Behind him, Shaun glanced at the rules of **HOOF, HOOF, SQUEAL, BLEAT.** Pig hoof crushed sheep hoof, and squeal was louder than bleat. There was no way the sheep could win. The game hadn't even started and the pigs were already cheating!

CHAPTER FOUR

GAME ON!

Chickens perched on the stone walls. One strutted back and forth with a tray of chicken feed around her neck. Timmy's Mum kicked her leg high in the air and shook two rustling pom-poms made from hay. The rabbits had been fluffier, but they had started to complain about being shaken in the air. She had stayed up all night making the new pom-poms, as well as a short skirt and a T-shirt with the words **GO, FLOCK** across the front. She beamed as the crowd cheered.

Meanwhile, Bitzer jogged around the field, blowing on his whistle and pointing at things. He had heard this was a big part of a referee's job.

The cheers became deafening. After whispering a few bleats to the huddled Flock, Shaun trotted to the flowerpot that marked the start of the obstacle course. His face looked grim and determined. In one hoof he clutched the tennis ball. As the crowd went quiet, he nodded at Bitzer: *Ready.*

Along the walls, sheep fans raised their legs or wings as they did the wave.

A mole commentator held a megaphone to his mouth. Every animal on Mossy Bottom Farm leaned forward, straining to hear as his tiny voice was magnified into a faint whisper: "Welcome, Bitzerball—I mean, Piggy Stomp fans. The first obstacle is the maze. The sheep captain must hop through the maze to the pen at the other end, avoiding the pigs. Oooh—he's off."

Bitzer had blown his whistle.

Like a flash, Shaun hopped toward the bales of hay that marked out the maze. Waiting to jump on him were three not-so-little pigs. They shouldn't be a problem, he thought. The pigs will be easy to hop around.

Squeeeeeee!

Shaun stopped. The pig captain was waving at Bitzer. Foul!

Bitzer flicked through the jumble of rules. Was it a foul? *Yes!* The **BITZERBALL** rules were still in the list. Players had to begin by waving their bottoms. His whistle peeped again. Shaun had to pay the penalty. Which was—he flicked pages again—ten points off and he had to complete the first obstacle with a bucket on his head.

Shaun groaned as the world went dark.

Remembering to wag his tail, he waited for
Bitzer's whistle again and then hopped away
in what he hoped was the right direction.
He could hear Timmy's Mum's muffled
cheerleading and pigs laughing. Gritting his
teeth, he hopped faster. He'd show them. . . .

Squeee!

Ooof. Shaun was flattened by a pig who had belly-slammed him to the ground. Fresh waves of laughter rolled across the meadow. With the bucket rattling around his ears, Shaun dragged himself out from beneath the pig and wobbled to his feet. Dizzily, hooves stuck out in front, he set off again, in the wrong direction.

Flock fans groaned. Hazel stepped forward, put both hooves to her mouth, and whistled. Shaun stopped, recognizing the sheepdog command. It meant *turn around*. Swiveling on the spot, he bounced away in a new direction. The pigs stopped chortling.

The mole lifted the megaphone and whispered again. "Great play from the Flock. After a rough start, they seem to be hitting their stride!"

Hazel's whistle cut through the air again. Peep, peep! *Go slightly to the left.* Peep-peep-peepetty-peep! *Straight ahead.* Peep! *Right, past the pig.* Peep, pee! *A little more to the right.*

Shaun heard a grunt as a pig slammed the empty space just behind him.

Peeep-poop! *That's good. Now watch out for the cowpat.* Peep-peepy-peep-pe-peep-pa-dum! *Stop, open the gate, go into the pen, and take the bucket off your head.*

After tossing the bucket aside, Shaun dropped the tennis ball into the flowerpot and grinned at the crowd.

"Ten points to the sheep, which, after their ten-point penalty, gives them a score of zero," murmured the mole commentator. "Now it's the pigs' turn."

The Flock lined up among the hay bales in the maze, ready to jump the pig captain. But Shaun knew he was far too big and strong for any of them to tackle; the Flock needed another plan, and quickly.

The pig captain tucked the tennis ball under his arm and then carefully waved his bottom at the referee.

Shaun groaned. He had been hoping that in the fierce heat of competition, the pig captain, too, would forget.

As Bitzer's whistle peeped, the bull snorted. Why are the farm animals making so much noise today?

Bitzer woofed an apology, but Shaun grinned. He'd just had a very good idea. He clicked his hooves to gather the Flock together and then whispered his plan. . . .

Bitzer blew his whistle again, a little more quietly this time.

"Oooooh . . . and the pig captain is off," yelled the excited mole commentator so loudly that the crowd could almost hear him. "He looks cool under pressure as he charges toward the end of the maze. The sheep haven't bothered to defend it, and he's going to make it through in record time. He's nearly there . . . but . . . wait . . . what's this?"

With all the players hiding in trees or behind walls, the bull soon got bored and, with a final snort, wandered back to his own field. Shaun jumped down from the wall and pushed the gate closed.

To groans from the pig supporters, Nuts pushed a wheelbarrow full of old clothes onto the field. It was time for the pig captain's penalty: **PIG IN A WIG.**

The pig captain stared at the clothes in the wheelbarrow: an old-fashioned pair of long, frilly knickers, a blue-and-white ruffled dress, and a wig. He crossed his arms and shook his head. No! He wouldn't do it.

Bitzer held up a paw. Did he want to forfeit the game?

The pig wheezed in anger. He jammed the wig onto his head.

Nuts fussed about, putting the finishing touches on the pig captain's outfit. He needed a handbag — *there* — and perhaps a hat would look nice perched on his curls. . . .

By the time Nuts had finished, even the other pigs were snorting. Their captain glared them into silence.

Chapter Five
THE DEATH-DEFYING **LEAP** OF SHEEP

"And with the score at zero-zero, it's time for the **PIG-SWILL SWAMP**," the mole commentator announced while the pig captain popped the tennis ball into his handbag. "An event where competitors sink or swim. First up is the pig captain. The swamp is five feet deep and filled with thick, oozy muck. All the players have to do is get from one side to the other."

The pig captain was already hopping toward the swamp. He landed in the mud with a squelch, and surfed across on his belly. Then, after barely pausing to catch his breath, he dropped the tennis ball into the flowerpot with a smug look at Shaun: *Beat that!*

Shaun's heart sank. That was another ten points for the pigs. They had chosen this obstacle well. Pigs loved mud, while sheep disliked getting their fleece dirty.

Shaun didn't have a hope of scoring, unless he could think of something clever. He racked his brains for a **BITZERBALL** rule that might help.

There was nothing . . . unless . . . unless. He thought about the Flock's original rules. A light went on in his head: *Shirley's rule!* If the Twins pushed Shaun in the wheelbarrow, he could use it as a boat to cross the mud bath!

It was brilliant!

The pigs were not happy, but there was nothing they could do about it. The rules

are the rules, Bitzer woofed, and Shaun can play this rule anytime he likes.

The wheelbarrow made it halfway across the **PIG-SWILL SWAMP** before — Squer-luppp — it squelched to a stop. The thick mud oozed through a hole in the bottom of the makeshift boat. Shaun covered the hole with a hoof, but another leak sprang up, then another. Slowly, the wheelbarrow began to sink. . . .

The last sounds Shaun heard before disappearing into the mud were the groans of the sheep supporters and the cheers of the pig fans.

A few minutes later, looking like a chocolate that had been left out in the sun, he dragged himself out of the **PIG-SWILL SWAMP** and shook mud from his ears.

"And that puts the pigs into the lead at ten points to zero," said the mole commentator.

Bitzer's whistle peeped again.

Shaun scratched his head. He was at the third flowerpot, which was now surrounded by bales of straw. Bitzer read the rules: players have five minutes to build a house from hay that will not blow down.

Shaun unfolded plans the pigs had

thoughtfully provided. Scrawled across the first page was a rough drawing of a wobbly-looking shack. A pig was looking out the window and blowing a fat raspberry.

Ignoring the pigs falling down laughing, Shaun scrunched up the drawing and tossed it over his shoulder. With a frown of concentration, he tugged on one of the bales, then gulped. It was almost too heavy to move.

"We're thirty seconds in," said the mole with a chuckle. "It looks like the Flock's captain could be in big trouble here."

Shaun put his shoulder against the bale and heaved. Slowly the bale slid into position. He had completed the first part of one wall.

"Two minutes left."

Determined not to be beaten, Shaun

dragged another bale into place, dripping sweat and fat blobs of sticky mud from the **PIG-SWILL SWAMP** onto the hay. He strained and heaved to cheers from the Flock fans, and slowly, slowly, he built his house.

Too slowly.

By the time the final whistle blew, Shaun had finished just two walls and half a kitchen.

"Ooooh, the sheep are going to lose points here," the mole shouted in a soft whisper. "Points can only be awarded for a completed house."

Shaun groaned. He still hadn't won a single point for the Flock team, and time was running out.

His groan turned to a yelp of despair as Bitzer blew his whistle again and the pig captain strode forward with a pencil tucked behind one ear and a tool belt strapped around his waist. He gave Shaun a smug squeal. We're natural builders. Straw, wood, bricks—pigs can build a house out of anything. . . .

The pig captain's house rose in a whirlwind of dust as Shaun looked on in shock.

It was a *beautiful* house. The pig captain made two columns on either side of the elegant front door and then added a small extension, useful for guests. A wide patio area curved around the side. There was also a garage and a shed for garden tools.

At that moment, a light breeze wafted over the meadow. The house swayed slightly. Shaun rubbed his chin. The pigs may be

great builders, but their houses usually failed to meet basic building regulations.

Bitzer looked down at his watch, checking the time. His whistle dangled from the clipboard. Shaun casually reached out and unhooked it.

The pig captain's time was up. Bitzer lifted up his clipboard, searching for the whistle. Shaun tried to look innocent, arms behind his back. Bitzer would have to improvise; he puffed his cheeks and blew out a high, piercing whistle.

The glorious structure collapsed in a crash of dusty straw. Bitzer frowned. The rules clearly stated that the house must be standing at the end of the challenge. Shaun held out the whistle, and Bitzer snatched it back. Peep! No points for the pigs in the House of Straw round.

The crowd went wild. Timmy's Mum high-kicked her way across the meadow, waving her hay pom-poms, until—

SPLOOSH!

"That round was a blow for the pigs in more ways than one," the mole commentator said. "They were looking for maximum points here, but the pig captain's charming house was structurally unsound and must therefore be disqualified."

Shaun grinned up at the pig captain, who scowled back from beneath the curls of his wig.

The pig captain oinked. His house might not have survived, but the pigs were still in the lead. Next, Shaun had to face him in the dash to the last flowerpot. Soon Shaun would be singing the **"PIGS, PIGS, PIGS"** song. . . .

Chapter Six
THE FINAL WHISTLE

Competition was heating up between the pigs and the sheep. As Shaun and the pig captain glared at each other, Bitzer coughed and jabbed a paw at the rules. The pigs' rules said that any team that failed to build a house had to pay a penalty in the next round.

Bitzer woofed. Both teams had failed, so BOTH teams would have to compete in the final race with an additional challenge decided by the other team.

Shaun smiled to himself, his mind already racing with ideas for a penalty. The pigs had obviously added the rule thinking that they would be safe.

Their captain flipped a page on the clipboard. A sneer broke out on his face as he pointed to the penalty the sheep would have to pay.

The whistle fell from Bitzer's mouth. Wide-eyed, he looked up at Shaun and shrugged. *Sorry, there's nothing I can do.*

Tired, muddy, and bruised, Shaun watched as the pigs pushed the Farmer's rusty old bicycle across the meadow. Flock fans started to boo, and a tingle of fear shivered down Shaun's spine.

His penalty for failing to build a complete house was the **DEATH-DEFYING LEAP OF SHEEP!**

The pig captain snickered. Or Shaun could always admit defeat and play the **SQUEALING PIGGY** card. . . .

Shaun shook his head. No, he would do the penalty, but first he had to decide on one for the pig captain. With a bleat, he beckoned the rest of the Flock over.

The Sheep went into a huddle. Whispers and giggles could be heard across the meadow. The rest of the farm animals watched in tense silence. What was the pig captain's penalty going to be?

Finally, the huddle split up. Hazel hurried away to the barn as Shaun trotted back to Bitzer. The pig captain's penalty would be the **PIGGYBACK RODEO.** He would have to finish the course carrying . . . a sheep.

Delight spread across the pig captain's face as he spotted Hazel trotting across the meadow, carrying a dusty saddle. She looked as light as a feather. He could carry her to the village and back and still win!

As he buckled the saddle onto the pig's back, Shaun shook his head. Hazel wasn't the rider. They heard a deep bleat behind them. The pig captain looked over his shoulder.

Shirley smiled at him, touching the brim of her cowboy hat in a friendly howdy.

As the pig captain's jaw dropped open, Shaun slipped a bridle over his head and handed the reins to Shirley. Giddyup!

"Wearing a wig and a fabulous gown, the pig captain will be ridden across the meadow to the final flowerpot," announced the mole.

The two captains took up positions at the starting line. A tennis ball in his mouth, Shaun peered over the handlebars of the bike. The score was zero to ten, and everything hung on this final race. All Shaun had to do was ride the bike across the meadow, use a plank ramp to jump over the Flock, and then make a dash for the last flowerpot and drop the ball inside it.

The pig, meanwhile, had to get to the flowerpot with Shirley on his back — a task that would demand stupendous strength and determination.

Bitzer blew his whistle. Peeeeeep!

And they were off. . . .

74

75

77

After Shaun dropped his tennis ball into the final flowerpot, his eyes slid shut with exhaustion.

Peeeeeeeeeeeeeeeeep! Peeep-peep-peep! Bitzer blasted his whistle. Shaun was the winner of this obstacle, making the **PIGGY STOMP** game a draw!

Shaun opened his eyes. The scoreboard stood at ten-ten. The cheers of Flock fans ringing in his ears, he staggered to his feet and breathed a sigh of relief. The Flock hadn't won, but at least they wouldn't have to sing **"PIGS, PIGS, PIGS"** for the next month.

He turned, blinking, as Bitzer's whistle sounded across the meadow again. The sheepdog jogged across the field, his pages of rules flapping away in the breeze.

Pigs were rolling oil drums across the meadow. Others were carrying long planks and heavy-duty springs over their shoulders. As Shaun watched, they started sawing and hammering the planks to make what looked like two springboards. What was going on now?

A second later, his question was answered by Bitzer, who arrived at his side and pointed out RULE 176C. It stated: A DRAW WILL BE DECIDED BY PIGS MIGHT FLY.

The pigs had one last trick to play.

Shaun stared from the springboards to the barn, where the pigs were painting a target on the wall. He gulped. Surely PIGS MIGHT FLY wasn't what he thought. . . .

Bitzer woofed: *Ready?*

Nervously, Shaun nodded. At his side, the pig captain squealed.

Bitzer peeped his whistle:

Oooohs and aaahs echoed around the farmyard as the two captains dashed, neck-and-neck, across the grass toward the springboards.

Shaun bounced onto his board with all his weight. He was catapulted into the sky, his arms and legs scrabbling at the air as he somersaulted toward the barn wall.

He heard a squeal of frustration and looked back to see that the pig captain had stumbled over Timmy, hit his springboard

awkwardly, and then bounced off at the wrong angle.

As Shaun sailed through the air, a smile lit up his face. With all the new rules the pigs had added, they had forgotten about the **TIMMY OBSTACLE.** Either team could ask Timmy to sit wherever they wanted on the field to trip their opponents—

SPLAT!

Shaun had hit the side of the barn. He blinked and looked around woozily. His fleece had caught on the rough surface of the barn wall, and he was hanging, spread-eagled, upside down.

Squeeeeeeeeeeeeeeeeeeeeeeeeeee . . .

The pig captain shot over Shaun's head. Missing the barn completely, the pig soared far, far into the sky, his stylish curls and frilly dress fluttering behind him.

. . . eeeeeeeeeee —

P.U.!

Shaun heard a distant squelch. It sounded as though the pig captain had landed in the manure heap. Shaun snickered and thought, For a pig, that probably counted as first prize.

The crowd flapped and clucked and bleated and squealed. Points were added to the blackboard. Shaun had secured ten points in **PIGS MIGHT FLY,** which meant that the Flock had won, twenty to ten! The commentator was almost bursting with excitement. Timmy's Mum waved her pom-poms as she high-kicked her way across the meadow.

"Bleat, bleat, bleat, bleat: who do we apprec-eee-eat?"

A few of the sheep pulled an exhausted and filthy Shaun down from the barn wall. With a cheer, they carried him on a victory lap of the meadow. Shaun was dazed but happy.

"And it's a **PIGGY STOMP** win for the Flock!" screamed the mole into his megaphone. Shaun cupped a hoof to his ear and could just make out the words, "The pig captain played brilliantly, except for ending up a total loser, and now the crowd has gone bonkers."

CHAPTER SEVEN
THE PIGS' PENALTY

As the first stars came out, Shaun leaned against the gate, happy. He could hear the disgruntled squeals of horrified pigs as they thrashed about in foaming sheep dip—their penalty for losing the game. Pigs hated baths!

Shaun grinned. The day had been far from boring, and now the pigs were squeaky clean.

A soccer ball bounced off his head. Shaun looked around and saw the ball rolling back to Bitzer's feet. Bitzer woofed, kicking it into the air with one foot and bouncing it from knee to knee. Did Shaun fancy a game?

Shaun thought about it for a second, but then shook his head. Maybe he should give **BITZERBALL**—and **PIGGY STOMP**—a pass for a while. The rules were far too complicated, and it would be a while before all his muscles stopped aching.

Brrrrrrrrriiiiiing.

They both jumped at the sound of the Farmer's alarm clock and turned toward the farmhouse.

Still in his pajamas, the Farmer threw the curtains open to take a deep breath of fresh morning air with a happy "Aaaaah" that turned into a confused "Huh?" when he saw the night sky . . . and then a "Bah." He jerked the curtains closed angrily and stomped back to bed. Shaun and Bitzer heard the ringing sound of the clock being shaken. A moment later, fresh snores drifted out the window.

Bitzer and Shaun looked at each other. Then Shaun's face split into a grin. "Heh, heh, heh," he snickered, passing the ball back to Bitzer and giving him a thumbs-up.

ACTIVITIES

HOW TO CREATE YOUR OWN GAME

MATERIALS

Colored pencils

A large piece of paper

Your imagination

My game is called _____

The object is to _____

It is for _____ players.

The rules: Rule 1: _____

Rule 2: _____

Rule 3: _____

Fill in your answers on a blank piece of paper.

Copy this diagram onto a blank piece of paper and then add your own rules and obstacles!

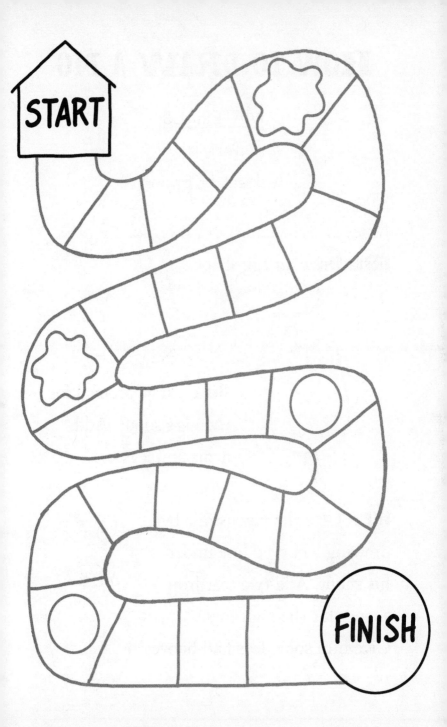

HOW TO DRAW A PIG

MATERIALS

Pencils

A sheet of paper

STEP 1 Draw an egg shape.

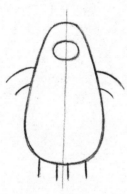

STEP 2 Draw an oval for the pig's snout. Add arms and legs.

STEP 3 Give the pig a smile by drawing a curved line under his snout. Add two teardrop shapes for the pig's ears. Give him some legs and hooves!

94

STEP 4 Add some chubby cheeks by drawing half circles on either side of the pig's face. Join his mouth to his snout.

STEP 5 Give your pig eyes, nostrils, and teeth. Then add some color!

Tales from Mossy Bottom Farm

FLOCK TO THE SEASIDE

An excerpt from
another new book in the series!

CHAPTER ONE
BIG DAY OUT

In the trailer behind the Farmer's car, Shaun and the Flock bounced along green and leafy country lanes on a hot summer's day. As swallows dipped and swooped around them, the sheep bleated and hung their heads over the sides of the trailer, enjoying the breeze and taking in the sights of the open road.

Shaun's favorite sight was the Farmer's bald head banging against the roof of the car to shouts of "Ooo-aaaargh!" and "Bah!"

every time the car hit a bump in the road. Beside the Farmer was Bitzer, his head sticking out the window and one paw on his hat to keep it from blowing away. His tongue fluttered in the wind like a pink flag.

Shaun held on tight as the wheels hit an especially big bump. The Flock bleated to one another. With every mile, their curiosity grew. Where was the Farmer taking them on such a beautiful day?

Timmy was dreaming of the seaside. Shirley hoped they were going out to lunch at a restaurant with a dessert cart so large that it took three waiters to push it. The Twins wanted to go to a rock festival to see their favorite band, **THE REVOLVING CUCUMBERS.**

Nuts was sure they were going to the theater. He'd even brought some chocolate-covered raisins he'd found sprinkled over the floor of the rabbit hutches to share during the intermission. He peered into the paper bag. The rabbits were crazy to leave perfectly good chocolate-covered raisins lying around like that.

Nuts's thoughts were interrupted by an excited bleat from Shaun, who was leaning over the side of the trailer and pointing a hoof. Through a gap in the trees, Nuts caught a glimpse of something that was deep blue, sparkling, and dotted with white. The Farmer wasn't taking them to the theater.

He was taking them to the seaside!

The Flock bleated delightedly as the car clanked over the top of a hill. The sea spread out before them, stretching to the horizon. Even better, in the distance were the striped tents, Ferris wheels, and roller coasters of an amusement park. The breeze smelled of cotton candy and sunblock.

Squeezing his eyes closed in concentration, Timmy reached into Shirley's fleece and pulled out a bucket and shovel. Reaching in again, he found a pair of floaties and a surfboard. Happy sheep beamed at one another. Shaun started three bleats for the Farmer: "Bleat, bleat-ooo-ooooo . . ."

The second bleat turned into a wail as the

an excerpt from *Flock to the Seaside*

car turned sharply. The Flock was thrown from one side of the trailer to the other and almost tipped out. Then, on two wheels instead of four, the car screeched through an open gate and skidded to a halt in a field.

"Bleat," finished Shaun in quiet disgust.

The meadow was filled with familiar sights. Farmers in muddy green coats and tall rubber boots stood sipping tea and eating sandwiches outside a small tent. Through the open flap of another tent, Shaun could see men poking an enormous squash and making notes.

There were stalls selling **BARRY STILES'S SHEEP DIP** and **HOOF-U-LIKE OINTMENT** and **DOCTOR ULCER'S PIGGIN' LOVELY PIG RUB**. A sign that read **THE GREAT PIDDLINGTON-ON-SEA ANNUAL FARM EXTRAVAGANZA** hung from the front of a trestle table. . . .

an excerpt from *Flock to the Seaside*